All Together Now!

by Susan Hood
illustrated by Cecile Schoberle

Scott Foresman

Editorial Offices: Glenview, Illinois • New York, New York
Sales Offices: Reading, Massachusetts • Duluth, Georgia
Glenview, Illinois • Carrollton, Texas • Menlo Park, California

We start out on a family walk.
It is a bright day.
All together now!

We see a deer.
We see a hawk.
All together now!

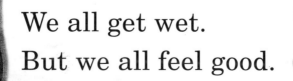

We all get wet.
But we all feel good.

We all get hugs.
We start out again.
All together now!

We see bugs.
Many, many bugs!
We slap them.

We start to climb a rock.
It is so high!
All together now!

We come up to a deep cave.
It is so dark.
All together now!

We all look in.
We feel so brave.
All together now!

We look around.
We see a bat.

We look around some more.
We see some tracks!
All together now!

We turn around.

We all turn back.
All together now!

13

We run and run and run!

All together now!

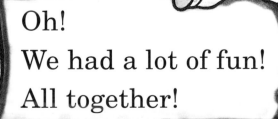

Oh!
We had a lot of fun!
All together!